Finlay MacTrebble and the Fantastic Fertiliser

Scoular Anderson

A&C Black · London

JUMBO JETS

First published 1995 by A&C Black (Publishers) Ltd
35 Bedford Row, London WC1R 4JH

Copyright © 1995 Scoular Anderson

ISBN 0-7136-4250-5

A CIP catalogue record for this book
is available from the British Library.

Photoset by Rowland Phototypesetting Ltd
Bury St Edmunds, Suffolk
Printed in Great Britain by
William Clowes Ltd, Beccles and London

CHAPTER ONE
A Few Facts About Finlay MacTrebble

Finlay MacTrebble had three nicknames.

NICKNAME NUMBER 1: Fiddly Fingers.
(This was what he was called at school.)
Finlay had fingers that couldn't keep still.
His fingers found things that no one else's
did. His fingers found bits of string or
springs or handy pieces of plastic.

His fingers found useful bits and pieces in
pockets, forgotten things in cupboards
and strange things at the back of sheds.

3

If there were things to be tightened or loosened or unwound, Finlay's fingers would find them.

Things quite often came to bits in Finlay's fingers – like other people's pens . . .

. . . or door handles . . .

. . . or garden gates.

NICKNAME NUMBER 2: Fixit Finlay.
(This was what he called himself.) Finlay
didn't worry too much about things
coming to bits in his fingers because he
was a brilliant fixer. If anything needed to
be fixed, Finlay would do it.

He was especially
brilliant at inventions.
He once hung a wet,
soapy blanket across
the garage door so
that the car would be
washed as it drove

in. And he was particularly pleased with
his invention of a cat dish that moved
around the kitchen. The idea was that the
cat would work up an appetite chasing
the dish around.

NICKNAME NUMBER 3: That Terrible MacTrebble. (This was what some other people called him.) Finlay was a friendly and helpful sort of boy. He liked to go and say hello to people around the village, but as far as they were concerned, Finlay always seemed to turn up just at the wrong moment. Like the time he turned up to find his  teacher sitting in her store-room reading a comic she had just confiscated.

Or the time he turned up to find the bank manager doing duck-impressions to the ducks in the park.

Finlay thought that 'Friendly Finlay' would be quite a good nickname to have. But if you asked a neighbour, like Colonel Wurmley-Eare, he would probably say:

That terrible MacTrebble boy... always popping up out of the shrubbery at inconvenient times.

You can hardly turn around when he's there in front of you!

Horrible, untidy sort of lad with a stupid grin on his face.

It was early on Saturday morning and Finlay was already fiddling. His mum had complained that one of the cupboard doors in the kitchen was difficult  to open and Finlay had had a brilliant fixit idea. He found a very long piece of string and tied one end of the string to the cupboard door. He tied the other end to the kitchen door. When someone opened the kitchen door then – hey presto! – the cupboard door would open too.

Finlay heard his dad coming downstairs.
He stood back to watch his brilliant idea in
action. When his dad opened the kitchen
door the cupboard door opened too.

9

Not only that, the cupboard door came right off its hinges and flew across the room. It almost knocked his dad out.

CHAPTER THREE

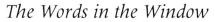

Finlay left the house and wandered down the road. He was annoyed that his dad had told him to go and do something useful. He was *always* being useful. The trouble was, no one liked his usefulness.

He stopped at the corner shop. There were often lots of useful things in the window, like air pumps and water pistols and cardboard tubes. Today he didn't see anything he could spend his pocket money on, but something else caught his eye. It was a row of notices stuck to the inside of the glass. At the top was a card which said:

DRIPTON FLOWER SHOW

AUGUST 15TH ~ PRIZEGIVING 4.30pm
All those wishing to exhibit
please contact the show secretary
COLONEL N. O. WURMLEY-EARE

Just below that was a piece of paper which said:

DINO'S DELICIOUS DOGS
DELIVERED TO YOUR DOOR!

Service starts August 15TH.
Dino's spicy hot-dogs (special old family recipe) will soon be brought to your home by our special delivery service.

phone 345220

Beside that was a small poster which said:

LATIN AMERICAN DANCING

TANGO ~ SAMBA ~ CHA-CHA ETC.

DEMONSTRATION and TUITION in the SCHOOL HALL

| AUGUST 15TH 3.30pm | ALL WELCOME FOR DETAILS CONTACT RAYMOND PLUGGE DRIPTON HAIR & BEAUTY SALON |

Well, there's a lot going on in the village. I'm sure Fixit Finlay could be a help to some of these people.

Finlay wandered back up the road thinking of useful ideas for flower shows, hot-dogs and Latin-American dancing. He couldn't wait to get home and start inventing. But by the time he reached the top of the hill, he felt quite thirsty – a visit to Miss Millyspeed was called for.

13

Old Miss Millyspeed was the only person in the village who didn't complain about Finlay's usefulness. She was always pleased to see him and often had a jug of home-made lemonade ready for him. Finlay had invented several things for her. There was the illuminated fly-swatter so she could swat flies in the dark. And a doormat which made a loud, rude noise when someone stood on it.

'AND . . .' Finlay explained at the time,

... this is the really BRILLIANT bit— you'll hear the noise and know *someone's* at your door so you won't jump out of your skin when the doorbell rings!

Finlay walked up the path to her house. He could see Miss Millyspeed standing in her sun-porch muttering to herself.

'Hi, Miss Millyspeed,' said Finlay. 'You look worried. What's the problem?'

'Just look at these!' said Miss Millyspeed, pointing to a row of large flowerpots. Each one had a little plant in it. Miss Millyspeed showed Finlay an empty seed packet.

MAMMOTH AMAZON LILIES

STAR BUY

HUGE BLOOMS, WONDERFUL SCENT— A SPECTACULAR DISPLAY IN ONLY A FEW WEEKS

They've had plenty of that, dear. I've watered them and talked to them every day. The Flower Show is today, you know. I don't think they're going to grow any bigger by four o'clock.

Miss Millyspeed poured Finlay a glass of lemonade. He drank it quickly because he had lots of things to do.

Maybe I can find something to make your plants grow.

Good boy. You have such good ideas. People don't realize that. I think you're undervalued.

Finlay liked the word undervalued. He thought about it all the way home.

CHAPTER FIVE

The Wicked Ways of Wurmley-Eare

Finlay didn't waste much time at home. He had been working on a very clever invention for several days and he was sure Colonel Wurmley-Eare would be very interested in it. He fetched it from his room and set out down the street towards the Colonel's house.

Colonel Wurmley-Eare was not a very friendly man. In fact, he was rather a nasty piece of work. As the Secretary of the Dripton Flower Show he expected to win first prize every year – and he always did because he cheated.

The Colonel never grew the plants himself. A few days before the flower show he went to a big garden centre some distance from the village. He searched for the plant with the glossiest leaves and biggest flowers.

He bought it, took it home and pampered it in his greenhouse. Then he entered it for the flower show, and it always won.

This year, things were different. He had seen his neighbour, Miss Millyspeed, carefully sowing seeds in her porch.

He even knew what they were. He had read the name on the packet through his binoculars:

'Hrmph! Never heard of them before,' he said to himself. Then some horrible thoughts struck him.

Suppose these lilies are mammoth.

Suppose they're covered in exotic blooms!

Suppose I can't find a plant in the garden centre to match a Mammoth Amazon Lily!

Suppose...

... old Millyspeed WINS!

The Colonel had a sleepless night worrying about this, but the following morning he had a brilliant idea: he would grow his own Mammoth Amazon Lilies. He would not be outdone by old Millyspeed. He went to the garden centre and searched the shelves for an identical packet of seeds.

Then he hurried home and planted them. Each day he checked on Miss Millyspeed's plants through his binoculars.

There was no doubt about it, although her plants weren't very big, they were still twice as big as his. He would have to take some drastic action. He *had* to win first prize at the flower show.

The Colonel spent another sleepless night.

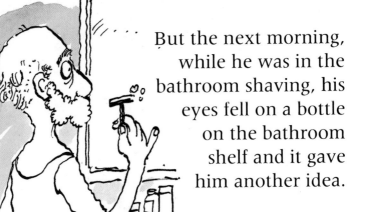

But the next morning, while he was in the bathroom shaving, his eyes fell on a bottle on the bathroom shelf and it gave him another idea.

He took the bottle out to his greenhouse. It was a bottle of:

TWINKLETOES FOOTWASH FOR HEALTHY FEET

He found a bottle in the greenhouse containing:

He emptied out the fertiliser and replaced it with Twinkletoes Footwash, then he put the cap back on the bottle and gave it a good shake.

This'll give old Millyspeed's lilies a bit of a shock!

Now all he had to do was think of a way of getting the bottle into Miss Millyspeed's porch.

23

The Colonel was just pondering on this problem when he saw someone's head beyond the garden gate.

'It's that Terrible MacTrebble boy,' he muttered. 'I hope he's not coming in here . . .'

Finlay certainly was coming in. He was also bringing a huge umbrella, with great difficulty, through the gate.

Hi there, Colonel. As you're the Secretary of the Dripton Flower Show, I wonder if you'd be interested in this useful gadget?

The Colonel looked at the umbrella. It had lots of tins and bottles hanging from it. They seemed to be full of water and were dribbling all over the path.

Finlay demonstrated. The cans and balloons hanging round the edge of the umbrella spattered water everywhere.

But it was too late. As Finlay whirled the umbrella around it decapitated several rose buds and they flew off over the hedge.

'I was only trying to be helpful,' said Finlay. He was just turning to go when he noticed the bottle of FIZZO FERTILISER FOR FABULOUS FLOWERS in the Colonel's hand.

'Why don't you take it to her?' said the Colonel, slyly.

'Thanks very much, Colonel,' said Finlay.

'Just one thing,' said the Colonel. 'It wouldn't be good if the Secretary of the Flower Show was seen trying to help other gardeners . . . know what I mean? Best not to mention where this came from, eh?' And he gave Finlay a wink.

The Colonel went off into his house humming to himself.

Finlay left the special plant-watering device at the garden gate as he went out. He was sure the Colonel would find it useful. Then he hurried home to work on a useful hog-dog idea he'd had for Dino.

It was nearly lunch time when Finlay set off from his home with his new invention. As he walked down the street, the Colonel called to him from his garden.

'Have you remembered the fertiliser?'

'Not yet, Colonel,' said Finlay. 'I'm a bit busy. I've got to go and see Dino first.'

The Colonel glanced at the pile of junk Finlay was carrying and scowled.

Dino was in the kitchen of his fish and chip shop preparing the first batch of his new family recipe spicy hot-dogs. As he stirred the sausage mixture, he sang happily:

Dino's Dog Deliveries,
Down Dashwood Avenue,
Up Heron Hill and Rudolph Road,
A service just for you!

He was just about to sing a second verse when something caught his eye. His mouth dropped open. A bright yellow hand appeared in the doorway. It waved at him then moved slowly into the middle of the room.

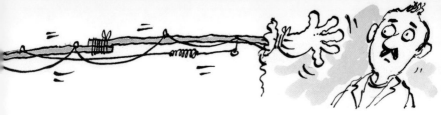

Dino could now see it was a rubber glove
on the end of a long pole. There were lots
of wires, strings and springs dangling
from the pole. The hand at the end
looked as if it was searching for
something.

It swung one way and bumped
against the light switch,
switching off the lights.

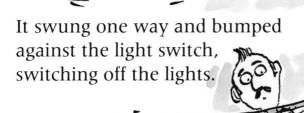

Then it swung back the other way and
down into Dino's sausage mix. Suddenly
it shot up and slapped
Dino on the face.

SPLAT!

Dino wiped sausage mix from his eyes.
Then he saw Finlay at the door.

'Hi, Dino!' said Finlay.

'Finlay MacTrubble, what are you
wanting? I'm busy. Go away!'

Finlay noticed that Dino had a large
cookery book propped up in front of him.

'I actually came to see if you'd be interested in this useful gadget I've invented?' said Finlay.

'No gadgets! I'm busy!' snapped Dino.

Finlay tried to demonstrate, but as he did so he knocked several plastic bottles off the table.

'Now see what you've done!' said Dino.

Finlay hurriedly dropped his gadget and picked up the bottles.

'Hey, look!' he said. 'I've got a bottle just like this one!' He took the bottle out of his pocket to compare them.

'OUT!' screamed Dino and he grabbed one of the bottles from Finlay.

Finlay shrugged and headed for the door. He left his handing-out device propped up against the wall as he was sure Dino would find it useful. Then he stuffed his bottle back into his pocket and headed home. What he didn't notice was that the bottle now in his pocket was:

And the bottle on Dino's table was filled with:

TWINKLETOES footwash for healthy feet.

CHAPTER SEVEN
A Little Too Lively Latin-American

During lunch, Finlay came up with a really brilliant idea for Raymond Plugge and his dance demonstration. He collected one or two things from his bedroom and headed for Dripton Hair and Beauty Salon.

Colonel Wurmley-Eare was in his garden as Finlay passed the gate.

'Well, boy,' grunted the Colonel. 'Have you been in to see Miss Millyspeed yet?'

'I haven't quite got round to it, Colonel,' said Finlay as he dashed past. 'I'm having so many useful ideas for other people!'

The Colonel looked at his watch and scowled. 'Well get a move on, boy,' he shouted, 'the show's only hours away.'

'I will,' Finlay promised, running down the street in the direction of Raymond's salon.

Dripton Hair and Beauty Salon was closed. Finlay pressed his nose against the window and peered under the blind. He could see Raymond at the rear of the shop. He was arranging a new display of beauty products and was busy stacking bottles and jars into a large pyramid.

Finlay went round to the back of the shop to look for another way in. Raymond had just finished his display and was checking his hair in a mirror when Finlay appeared at the back door. He was carrying a very odd-looking mop.

'Hi, Mr Plugge,' said Finlay, cheerfully.

Raymond Plugge whirled round.
He covered his head with his hands.

'We're closed!' said Raymond Plugge.
He was now very red in the face.
He snatched a wig from a chair and
pulled it on quickly.

Raymond muttered something about the
MacTrebble boy always turning up at the
wrong moment then he said aloud,

If I could just have a moment of your time, Mr Plugge. I've got an invention here that I'm sure will come in very useful for your Latin-American dance demonstration.

Finlay held up his mop with the fluffy end pointing upwards. There was a scarf pinned below the mop-head. There were two pieces of plastic drainpipe tied to the mop handle.

'It's a dance demonstration partner,' explained Finlay. 'Imagine the mop is your partner and the pipes are her legs . . .'

43

Finlay waltzed with the mop down the
length of the salon . . .

. . . but as he turned, the mop swung
round and hit Raymond's pyramid of
bottles and jars. Down they came with a
crash. Finlay landed on the floor in the
middle of them.

44

'Now see what you've done!' wailed Raymond Plugge.

'Don't worry, I'll help you put them back,' said Finlay.

'No you won't. You've done enough damage,' said Raymond. 'I want you out of here THIS INSTANT!'

Finlay picked himself up and made for the door. He turned and came back.

'I've dropped a bottle that was in my pocket,' he said, gazing at the bottles on the floor.

Ah, here it is!

He picked up a green bottle and stuffed it in his pocket. He left his mop dance demonstrator by the door as he went out. He was sure Raymond would find it useful.

Raymond carefully rebuilt his display of
bottles and jars. He just had enough time
to go upstairs to his flat and have a
shower before the dance demonstration,
so he decided to
treat himself to
something from
his display.
He picked up
a bottle of:

TARZAN
TOILETRIES
FOR
MEN
AFTER SHOWER
TALC

At least, that's what he thought it was. The bottle looked the same as all the others, but if he had read the label he would have seen:

Meanwhile, Finlay was heading for Miss Millyspeed's to give her the fertiliser, but what he now had in his pocket was a bottle of:

As Finlay arrived at Miss Millyspeed's gate the Colonel was just leaving for the Flower Show.

'I'm here at last, Colonel,' said Finlay.

'About time too,' grunted the Colonel, hoping the stuff in the bottle would have an instant reaction.

Miss Millyspeed was standing in her porch looking at her Amazon Lilies.

Hi, Miss Millyspeed. How are your plants?

49

Finlay took the bottle out of his pocket and read out the instructions on the back.

For that glossy, healthy look, apply one capful, rub well in then rinse thoroughly.

'Very odd instructions,' said Miss Millyspeed, 'but I suppose it's one of those modern fertilisers.'

Finlay poured a capful on to each plant then, just for extra health, he gave them each another capful. He rubbed the liquid all over the leaves then he gave them a good rinse with Miss Millyspeed's watering can. As he rinsed, a great froth rose up. The plants began to disappear under a blanket of bubbles.

So while the plants fizzed, Miss Millyspeed took Finlay inside to have some lemonade.

CHAPTER NINE

Rocketing Dogs Due to the Terrible MacTrebble

Dripton Village was a very quiet place. Nothing much out of the ordinary happened there except, perhaps, when Finlay MacTrebble tried to be useful. But this particular day of Finlay's helpful ideas was about to have some strange effects . . .

Dino had spent hours making his new family-recipe spicy sausages for his hot-dogs. However, without knowing it, he had seasoned them with large amounts of Twinkletoes Footwash.

As he carried the sausages out to his van, he tripped over something and almost dropped the lot.

'Stupid!' he cried, kicking Finlay's hot-dog server across the yard. He was still seething with rage as he drove across town to his first stop.

Dino parked his bright new van at the corner of Dashwood Avenue and put on his first batch of sausages to cook. Then something very strange happened.

Just as the sausages were browning nicely
one of them exploded in a shower of red
stars. Then another shot out of the pan
and across the road like a rocket trailing
blue smoke. Soon, sausages were leaping
and whirling all over the place, crackling
like fireworks. All down the street people
were coming to their windows to watch.

CHAPTER TEN
A Spicy, Twitchy Tango

Meanwhile, Raymond Plugge had just finished taking a long, long shower. It helped him forget Finlay MacTrebble. He combed his wig and set it on his head. Then he sprinkled TARZAN TALC all over his body.

Mmm, nice, spicy smell!

At least, that's what he thought it was. The bathroom was so steamy that he didn't see that it was, in fact, REELY-HOT SAUSAGE SPICE.

Raymond hurried into the bedroom to dress. As he came down from his flat, he tripped over Finlay's dance demonstration partner which was propped up against the salon door. He kicked the thing in a fit of temper and went very red but he had calmed down by the time he reached the school.

Half an hour later, he escorted Sharon on to the floor of the school hall. They were about to demonstrate the tango. Just as the music started, Sharon let out a loud sneeze. She was sure it had been caused by Raymond's aftershave or whatever he was wearing. Raymond, on the other hand, had a strange itchy feeling down his spine, and his armpits felt as if they were on fire. He wondered if he had used too much TARZAN TALC.

Sharon couldn't control her sneezing and Raymond couldn't control his itching. It was the strangest, twitchiest tango the audience had ever seen.

Back at Miss Millyspeed's, Finlay had just finished his third glass of lemonade.

'I can smell a strong perfume all of a sudden,' said Miss Millyspeed.

'So can I,' said Finlay.

'It's coming through the front door,' said Miss Millyspeed.

They got up and went into the porch.

The Mammoth Amazon Lilies had become really mammoth in the space of half-an-hour. Their leaves had grown as big as dinner-plates. The stems had almost reached the roof. Flowers as big as lampshades wafted strong perfume in every direction.

'You're bound to win the flower show with one of these,' said Finlay excitedly.

'But it's too late, dear,' said Miss Millyspeed. 'They will be judging at this very moment.'

'We'd get there in time if we ran,' said Finlay.

'Not with my poor legs,' said Miss Millyspeed.

Then Finlay caught sight of a wheelbarrow in the garden. Before Miss Millyspeed knew what was happening, Finlay had brought the barrow to the door and pushed her into it.

He chose the largest Amazon Lily and
plonked it on her lap. Then they were off!

Miss Millyspeed was light and it was
downhill all the way so they were at the
village hall in no time. Miss Millyspeed
kicked open the doors with her feet and
they rushed into the hall.

The wheelbarrow screeched to a halt
right in front of the judge who was just
about to pin the first prize label
on Colonel Wurmley-Eare's flower.

The judge looked at Miss Millyspeed's
Mammoth Amazon Lily in amazement.
She had never seen anything like it. She
stepped forward and awarded it first
prize. All the people in the hall burst out
clapping. All except Colonel Wurmley-
Eare who looked as if he was going to
explode. He marched out of the hall and
up the street. He was just turning into his
garden when he tripped over Finlay's
umbrella watering device at his gate.

CHAPTER TWELVE

A Funny Finish to Fixit Finlay's Useful Day

Meanwhile, Dino had rushed back to his shop in embarrassment after the exploding hot-dog event. He made another batch of sausages, this time with the right ingredients. It turned out that the sausage fireworks had been a great advert and people queued up to buy the new hot-dogs.

Raymond and Sharon's strange dance had been successful, too. Everyone in the hall signed up for dancing lessons. They especially wanted to learn the exciting new tango.

As Miss Millyspeed and Finlay walked home from the Flower Show, they talked about what had happened.

'I think it was probably my CASTIRON TONIC FOR COUGHS AND COLDS,' said Miss Millyspeed. 'It was horrible stuff the doctor gave me so I emptied it into the flowerpots!'

They both laughed all the way up the road and Finlay was glad it had been a really *useful* sort of day.